Dawn Watch

Groundwood Books / Douglas & McIntyre
720 Bathurst Street, Suite 500, Toronto, Ontario M5S 2R4
Distributed in the USA by Publishers Group West
1700 Fourth Street, Berkeley, CA 94710

We acknowledge for their financial support of our publishing program the
Canada Council for the Arts, the Government of Canada through the Book
Publishing Industry Development Program (BPIDP), the Ontario Arts
Council and the Government of Ontario through the Ontario Media
Development Corporation's Ontario Book Initiative.

ONTARIO ARTS COUNCIL
CONSEIL DES ARTS DE L'ONTARIO

National Library of Canada Cataloging in Publication
Pendziwol, Jean E.
Dawn watch / by Jean E. Pendziwol; pictures by Nicolas Debon.
ISBN 0-88899-512-1
I. Debon, Nicolas II. Title.
PS8581.E55312D38 2004   jC813'.54   C2003-907329-7

The illustrations are done in Pelikan "Plaka" casein paints
on Arches watercolor paper.

Design by Michael Solomon
Printed and bound in China

To Dad, with love. In memory of
dawn watches shared; in anticipation
of dawn watches to come.
J P

To Paul, Lisa and Nélina
N D

Dawn Watch

Jean E. Pendziwol

Pictures by

Nicolas Debon

A Groundwood Book

Douglas & McIntyre

Toronto Vancouver Berkeley

It was the deepest hour of night — a time when I was usually in my bunk sleeping, with the sails neatly stowed in their bags and the boat anchored and resting gently in a sheltered calm cove.

But not tonight.

Tonight we had to cross Lake Superior to Sault Ste. Marie and make landfall in daylight. That meant we had to sail all night.

It was my turn to take a shift with Dad.

We were on the dawn watch, when the night seems blacker and the air colder, before the sun begins to warm the edges of day.

I climbed through the companionway and stepped into the cockpit breathing deep breaths of crisp, cold air. Dad was a black shadow adjusting the trim of the sails. He handed me a rope and I twisted it around the cleat in a figure-eight pattern.

I knew that the first thing we had to do
when our watch began was plot our position
and mark it in the log book.

Dad said, "We need to know where we
are all the time."

It was my job to watch for ships and lights and land and logs, floating lost on the great inland sea. The autopilot's job was to steer the boat.

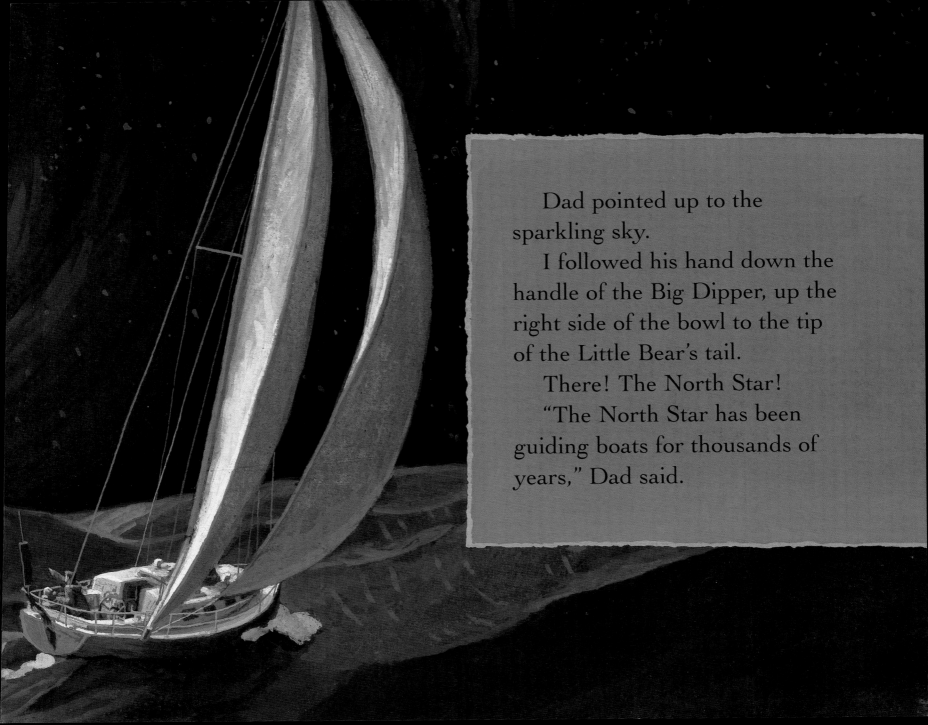

Dad pointed up to the
sparkling sky.

I followed his hand down the
handle of the Big Dipper, up the
right side of the bowl to the tip
of the Little Bear's tail.

There! The North Star!

"The North Star has been
guiding boats for thousands of
years," Dad said.

He checked our speed and the autopilot, then disappeared into the cabin below where the rest of the crew slept, until it was their turn to take a watch.

I was alone on the sea.

I snuggled into my orange float-coat. My feet dangled off the seat. Stretching my legs, I touched my toes to the floor of the cockpit.

The boat pitched
and I gripped a
cleat to keep from
sliding off the seat.
It was cold.
And I was alone
on the sea.

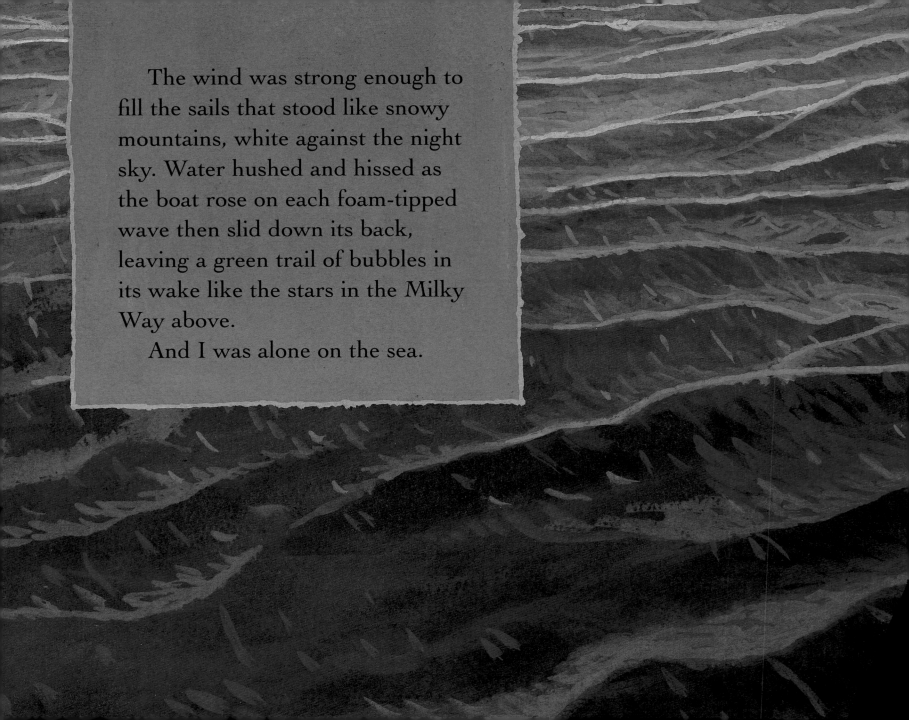

The wind was strong enough to
fill the sails that stood like snowy
mountains, white against the night
sky. Water hushed and hissed as
the boat rose on each foam-tipped
wave then slid down its back,
leaving a green trail of bubbles in
its wake like the stars in the Milky
Way above.

And I was alone on the sea.

I watched as the
waves turned into pirate
ships that crept closer on
silent sails, and monsters
reached wet, black
hands toward the boat,

and huge rocky islands appeared from the
depths of nowhere, and wooden rowboats
from sunken ships floated up and up…
I blinked and saw only waves.

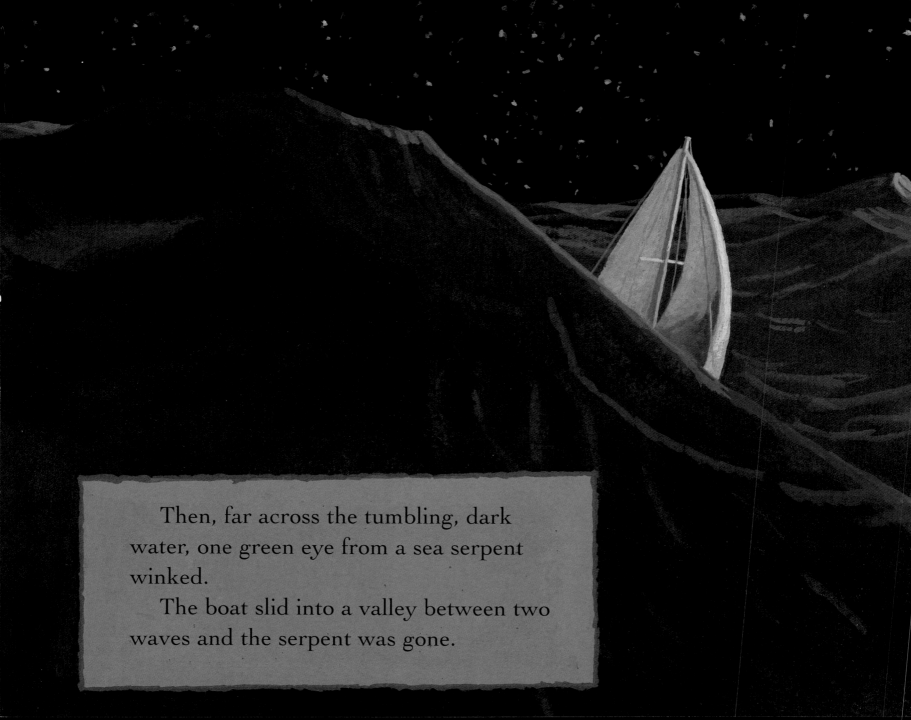

Then, far across the tumbling, dark
water, one green eye from a sea serpent
winked.

The boat slid into a valley between two
waves and the serpent was gone.

Another swell rolled beneath the hull
and there was the green eye again.

High above, Northern Lights
danced iridescent green across the
inky sky. A gust of wind snapped
a line against the main sail and we
heeled ever so slightly.

Still the serpent winked.

Sound the alarm! All hands on
deck! Man the battle stations!
Douse the lights!

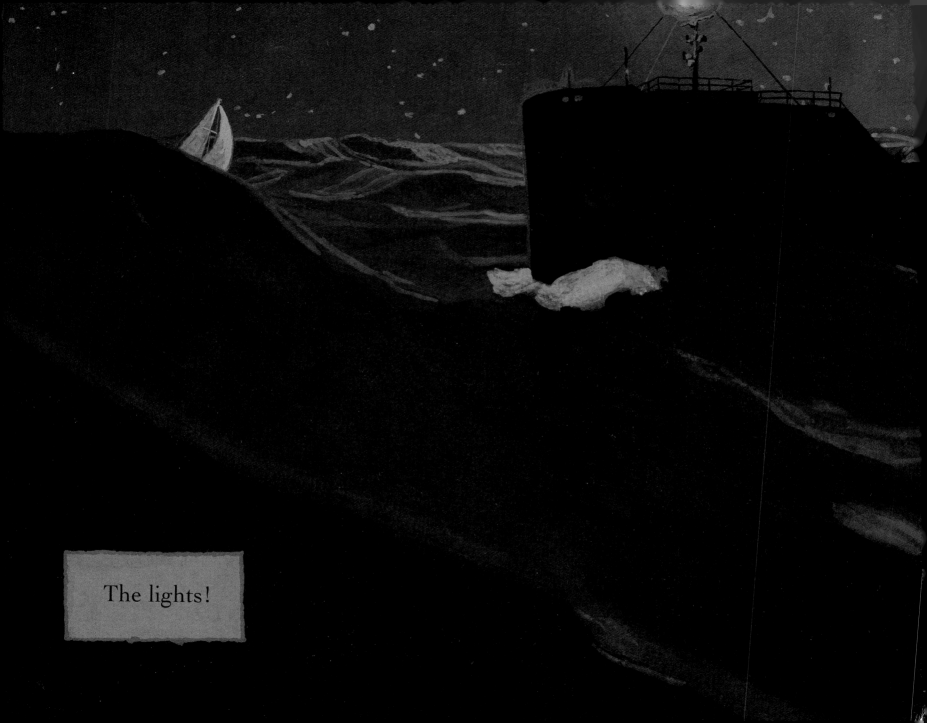

The lights!

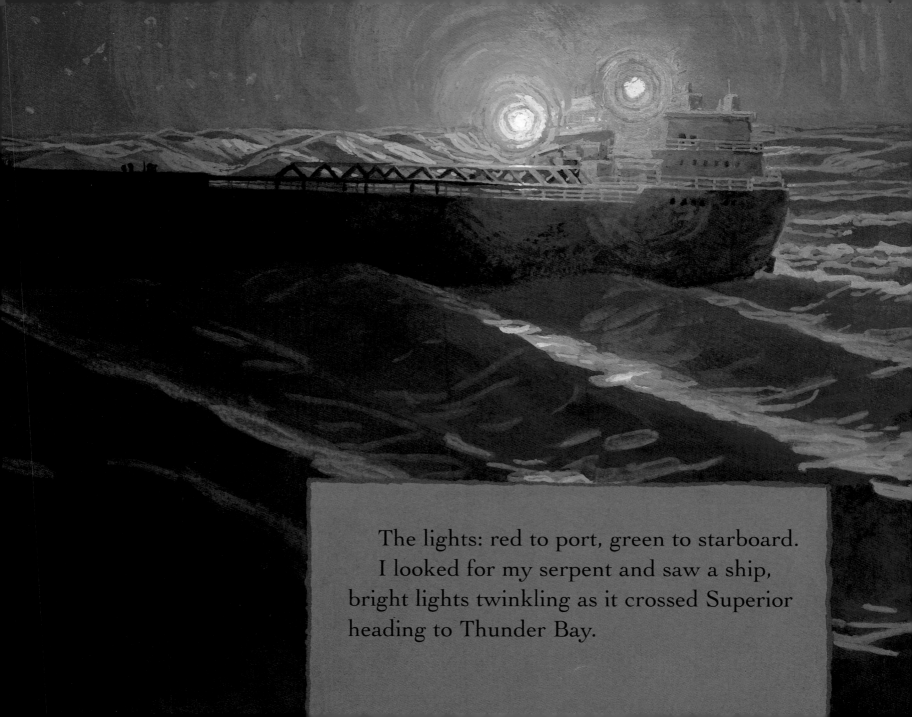

The lights: red to port, green to starboard.
I looked for my serpent and saw a ship,
bright lights twinkling as it crossed Superior
heading to Thunder Bay.

The ship-to-shore radio
crackled as Dad appeared.
I pointed to the ship.
He handed me a mug of
hot chocolate and told me that
I was a good first mate.
I sipped it quietly, the
steam warming my nose.

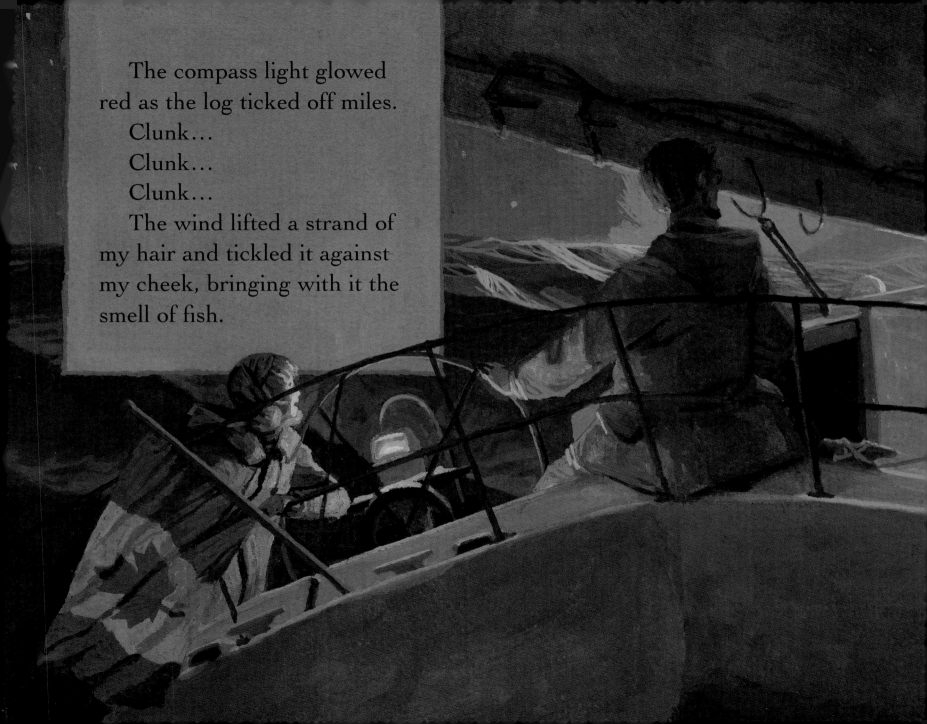

The compass light glowed
red as the log ticked off miles.
Clunk…
Clunk…
Clunk…
The wind lifted a strand of
my hair and tickled it against
my cheek, bringing with it the
smell of fish.

Dad touched my arm and pointed to the bow.

The horizon had begun to glow orange and pink streaked with purple haze, as the last pieces of the night sky were drawn back like a blanket, and the stars began to fade.

He handed me the binoculars
and there was land, bumpy and low,
a black line between sky and sea.

The clock chimed and
sleepy faces appeared.
The dawn watch
was over.